BABY'S BOOK

ILLUSTRATED BY BOB SMITH

A GOLDEN BOOK • NEW YORK

Western Publishing Company, Inc.
Racine, Wisconsin 53404

THE LITTLE GOLDEN BOOKS
ARE PREPARED UNDER THE SUPERVISION OF

MARY REED, Ph.D.

ASSISTANT PROFESSOR OF EDUCATION
TEACHERS COLLEGE, COLUMBIA UNIVERSITY

A COMMEMORATIVE FACSIMILE EDITION PUBLISHED ON THE OCCASION OF

THE 50TH ANNIVERSARY OF LITTLE GOLDEN BOOKS

Good morning, Kitty-cat.
Have you seen Tommy?

It's time for his bath,
but there's no baby in this tub;

Here's his comb and here's his brush,
soap and towels, rub-a-dub!

Here's an orange for his breakfast;
't will be ready in a minute.

Here's a cup; here's Tommy's chair,
but Tommy isn't in it.

Here's his spoon,
and here's his plate,

A bowl of cereal;
but Tommy's late.

Good morning, Bow-wow,
Have you seen Tommy?

Here are Tommy's blocks.

Here's his bouncing ball;

Here's a pretty box;
here's his old rag doll.

Good morning, Bluebird.
Have you seen Tommy?

When Tommy goes out walking,
he wears his coat and hat.

He has a pair of new shoes,

A baseball and a bat.

Let's go look in the sandpile
and see if Tommy's there.

I see his pail and shovel,
don't see Tommy anywhere.

Tommy has a garden rake;
Tommy has a hoe
and a little spade to dig the earth
and make the flowers grow.

Good morning, Butterfly.
Have you seen Tommy?

Let's give this big, red apple

To old Horsie at the gate.

Piggy wants his breakfast, too,
and doesn't like to wait.

Good morning, Moo-cow.
Have you seen Tommy?

There go the ducks to take a swim,

And here's the pond they dabble in.

Look: here comes our Bunny Rabbit.
Hop and nibble, ... funny habit.

*Would you like
this leaf, Rabbit?*

Or this one?

Or this one?

The white hen and her chickies
scratch for breakfast in the grass;

And pretty roses nod their heads
as fluffy chicks run past.

Here's the door. Let's go inside.
There are lots of places we haven't tried.

Good morning, Teddy Bear.
Have you seen Tommy?

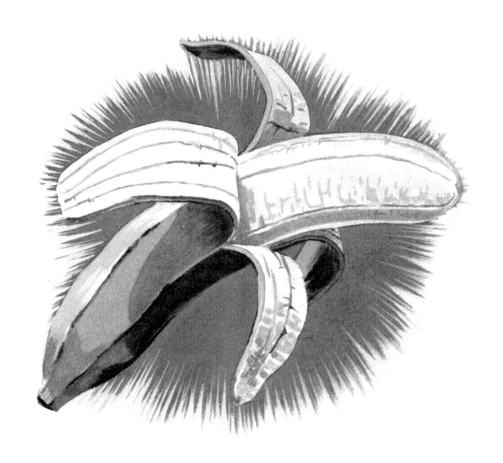

A ripe banana,
all yellow and sweet—
Here's something
Tommy just loves to eat.

Here is Tommy's kiddie car.

Here are Tommy's train

and all his tiny automobiles.

Here's his new airplane.

Let's ask the telephone.
Hello! Hello! Have you seen Tommy?

"It's time to get up," says the clock,
"And I haven't seen Tommy,
tick-tock, tick-tock!"

Here's a pillow for his head.
Let's go look in Tommy's bed.
Why, there's Tommy!